IKE AND MAMA AND THE ONCE-A-YEAR SUIT

To Sabilah
& Tasnim —

So nice to have
you visit me. I hope
we'll see you again.
Love —
Carol

Carol Snyder
November 20, 1992

IKE and MAMA
~ and the ~
Once-a-year Suit

by Carol Snyder

drawings by Charles Robinson

COWARD, McCANN & GEOGHEGAN, INC.

New York

Library of Congress Cataloging in Publication Data
Snyder, Carol.
  Ike and Mama and the once-a-year suit.
  [1. Mothers and sons—Fiction 2. Shopping—Fiction]
I. Robinson, Charles. II. Title.
PZ7.S685171k   [Fic]   77-21429
ISBN 0-698-20436-0

Designed by Cathy Altholz

Printed in the United States of America

Contents

I dedicate this book with love
to Mickey, Amy, and Linda,
my "encouragement mavens,"
and with thanks to
family and friends for sharing
their memories and knowledge.

～ 1/Ike in a Hurry

"Ike, hurry!*" said Mama.*

The canary chirped and the teapot steamed. They seemed to say "hurry."

"Coming, Mama." Ike shivered as a March-morning chill zigzagged through his body. He sidled closer to the open oven. Mama had just put some more coal in the stove. The kitchen floor was so cold. Ike carefully warmed his feet, lifting and balancing near the oven door. Then he pulled on his black stockings and buckled his bulky knickers.

The knickers bulged. They were his father's old suit pants, cut down and baggy. Ike thought warm woolen thoughts, because today was special. This was not any old no-school Sunday. Today was the Sunday before Passover, the Sunday of the once-a-year suit. And this year, 1918, Ike Greenberg would not just wait outside the Stanton Street stores. This year he, too, would "try on." Today Ike would buy his first suit, and it had to be a suit that would last all year. He wanted a blue suit—a nighttime-blue suit—that would fit perfectly for Passover this spring and still fit at Yom Kippur next September.

"Ike, stop dreaming. *Hurry.* We must be at the Third Avenue El train by eight-thirty."

"Why, Mama?" Ike buttoned his shirt.

"It's part of my special plan," Mama said, and she reached for a glass and poured in some freshly brewed tea. "Too strong," she said as she added steaming water from the kettle.

Ike could hardly wait to see Mama in action, to learn her special plan. She was known as a clothing maven, an expert!

"And Ikey, don't forget to wear your garlic bag. You don't need the flu. You need only a suit!" Mama chuckled at her joke as she pinched Ike's cheek lovingly. But getting the flu was no joke. These days everyone on East 136th Street in the Bronx wore a canvas bag filled with garlic: the bag, tied on a string and hung around the neck, was supposed to keep the flu away. Mama glanced out the kitchen window. She put a piece of sugar between her teeth and sipped the tea. Warming her hands on the glass, she seemed to enjoy the sweetness of each sip of tea as it passed through the sugar. Then she opened the window that looked onto the street. Ike's first cousins Sammy and Dave were already waiting on the stoop, wiggling with new-suit excitement.

"Davie, Sammy, tell the other boys to hurry," Mama yelled. "We must leave in five minutes, for sure." Mama put her glass in the sink and reached into the corner of the kitchen for the broom. She held the wooden handle high in the air and tapped three times on the ceiling. Then she turned the broom over and tapped three times on the floor.

The neighbors on East 136th Street were ready for Mama. For once-a-year suits everyone knew Mama needed both her hands and her mind free. So Ike's lit-

tle sister, Bessie, was eating porridge at
Aunt Sadie's, across the hall. And lunch
she'd have at Mrs. Mantussi's, downstairs. Supper, too, was being cooked. Mrs.
Weinstein, from upstairs, was in charge
of that. Yes, the neighbors were ready,
but people said Manhattan's Stanton

Street shopkeepers were never ready for Mama, *ever!*

Mama put the broom back in the corner. Downstairs a window was banged open and Mrs. Mantussi stuck her head out.

"We go," Mama called, leaning out the window.

"I wish you luck, Eva. You'll need it. Such expensive suits this year; you'll never get them for our price."

Mama smiled. "We will see," she said.

The window rattled open above and another head, Mrs. Weinstein's, looked down. "Morton's on his way downstairs with the money. Remember, I don't have a penny more to spend."

"On this block," muttered Mama, "who does?"

Mama closed the window, threw a black coat around her, and started toward the door.

"Hurry! The boys must be at the stoop already, and shush, Ikey, don't slam the door. Papa is sleeping, still. A man who works nights pressing clothes at a factory must get some sleep, too. No?"

"I'm coming," Ike said, closing the door quietly. Ike dashed around Mama, down three flights of stairs. Outside, his jacket blew open.

Mama followed, huffing and muttering, "*Oy!* Button up, Ikey."

Ike was too excited. He wanted to tell all the boys on the crowded stoop about the suit he would choose. Ike could see the Third Avenue Elevated tracks three blocks away. He could even see the roof of the firehouse, his favorite place. He cleared a path for Mama as he raced down, taking two steps at a time.

Neither Mama nor Ike had noticed the bag of garlic still hanging from the doorknob in the kitchen.

∼ 2/Ike's Worry

Ike looked down. The stoop was crowded with kids—all waiting for Mama. Every step held at least two bodies, and Ike's first cousins Sammy and Dave were tossing Tony Golida's cap in the air. Danny Mantussi, from downstairs, was hanging on to an iron handrail, and James Higgins and Morton Weinstein, from upstairs, sat huddled together. Ike's second cousins Sol and Bernie were there, too.

"Count heads, Ikey," Mama said.

"Nine, counting me," Ike answered.

"We are all here," Mama said, and she patted Ike's head gently.

"Let's go," Ike called to the other boys, "hurry!"

As the group walked down East

136th Street, a window screeched open and a head stuck out.

"Mrs. Greenberg! Could you maybe take Herbie, too?"

"Certainly, Mrs. Friedman," Mama answered.

"Eva Greenberg," another voice shouted. "Up here. Could Joey go with you?"

"Certainly," Mama called back above the clicking noise made by the hooves of a passing milk-wagon horse on the cobblestone street.

"Ikey," Mama called, huffing as she walked and talked, "we are almost at the train. Collect from each boy their five-dollar bill."

Ike started to run to the front of the group when Mama called, "And tell them to get their carfare ready, too. They are not to sneak under the turnstile, tell them."

"Okay, Mama," called Ike. The words trailed over his shoulder as he dashed away. No garlic bag slapped at his neck, but Ike did not notice.

Mama held a small purse. She took

out carfare for herself and Ike. "Sammy," she called. "Here, darling, run ahead and take care of the fares. *Oy*, hurry, children," Mama said. "I think I hear the train."

"Here, Mama," said Ike, weaving in and out to get near her. He handed her ten five-dollar bills.

She counted them and stuffed them into her purse, where another five-dollar bill peeked out. "Good," said Mama, "we are eleven boys now."

As the train roared and screeched to a stop, doors opened and Mama's army marched on board. Sammy and Dave went in first, followed by Tony and the towering Danny Mantussi. James Higgins and Morton Weinstein, Bernie and Sol, Herbie and Joey, were next, and breathless Jack, Robert, and Patrick waved three five-dollar bills, muttering, "Our mother said we could go, too." Mama took their money and tucked it into her purse. She stepped into the train, grabbing Ike's hand as he leaped in.

The train doors rolled shut. *"Oy,"* Mama moaned as she sat down on the straw seat and tucked the purse safely inside her blouse.

"Seventy dollars," Ike whispered to her, his forehead wrinkled with worry. "That's a lot of money."

"Shush, my darling one," said Mama, hugging him to her.

The train smelled like the inside of school, Ike thought as the Bronx whizzed by the windows. Sheets and quilts were flying like flags from the apartment windows. Fire escapes with ice boxes, plants, and chairs on them were a blur as the train picked up speed. Bicycles raced past horse-drawn carriages on the streets below.

The boys wiggled with anticipation. "I'd like a brown suit with stripes," Sol said. His voice shook with each bump of the train.

"I'm getting a black suit," Tony said. "I'll be the handsomest in church Easter Sunday."

"I want a nighttime-blue suit," Ike said, "like the fire chief's." Every day, the fire chief waved to Ike from the firehouse, and Ike happily waved back. Oh, Ike could feel the blue suit and smell it right now. He glanced at Mama, hoping she was listening to him. I listen to

Mama, he thought, so of course Mama will listen to me.

Mama looked at the advertisement pictures and patted her blouse.

"A beautiful blue suit," Ike said, again, just in case, and he patted his shirt. Then he felt all over his shirt. Something was missing. There was no string around his neck and nothing hung outside his shirt, or inside. The string and the bag of garlic must still be hanging on the kitchen doorknob. Oh, no! Ike thought. I *didn't* listen to Mama.

The straw train seat stuck him. He wiggled over to another spot and tried to forget the missing garlic. He thought about his dream suit instead. He wondered what he would do if he couldn't find a nighttime-blue suit.

"One thing," Mama said, and she pointed a short fat finger.

Ike knew each boy thought her finger was pointed at him.

"Do not say you like it about *any* suit." Her eyes looked at each serious face and squirming body. "Don't *look* like you like a suit, even. Not a smile in the mirror. Not a wink. Just try on. And

when I say we go, we *go!* That is part of
the special plan. So, *kinder,* children,"
Mama added, "no one wants to spoil a
special plan, right? Of course, *right.*" She
answered her own question. Not a single
boy dared to look away from Mama's
piercing blue eyes.

Anyway, everyone knew Mama. When Mama *said,* you listened, even though she was only four feet seven; even if at ten you were as tall as Mama, like Ike; even though she never raised her voice. Sometimes she never even said a word. She just raised her eyebrows and her blue eyes sparkled "Mama trouble"! Everyone listened to Mama: other kids, shopkeepers. But Ike had *not* listened. Ike thought of the missing garlic bag. Not listening to Mama was unheard of. Not listening to Mama was unthinkable. Not listening to Mama was uncomfortable. And worse yet, what if Mama didn't listen to him? What if she made him get a suit he didn't like? A suit that scratched and itched?

~ 3/Mama in Action

Stanton Street was already getting crowded. Shopkeepers were cranking open striped canvas awnings and salesmen were sweeping the sidewalk. A motorcar rumbled down the street, beeping a warning. A woman waved her black oilcloth shopping bag at the driver and scurried down the street.

"Yes," sighed Mama, "sweeping means we are on time. We will be the first customer at Miller's Clothiers. That is important!"

Mama needed to catch her breath, so the boys all stopped to watch the puller-inners, the coaxers. They were well-dressed salesmen in sample suits. They stood next to the shop windows looking like manikins until a person stopped to

look. Then they sprang into action.
When Mama looked in the window dis-
play at Miller's, the puller-inner put an
arm like a hook around her shoulders.

"Come inside," he said. "Have *I* got
a suit for your son."

The store was empty when Ike and Mama stepped inside and full by the time Mama's army had entered. It was a narrow store lined with racks of suits. A big three-way mirror filled one corner, with curtained cubicles nearby. A strong smell of oiled wood hung in the air. The polished wood floors gleamed the information that this was a fine store. Naturally, Mama was a clothing maven, an expert. She knew the best!

A gray-haired shopkeeper greeted Mama and sent the puller-inner out again. The shopkeeper was dressed in a gray and black pin-striped suit, a perfect fit. He had a wart on one side of his nose that wiggled when he spoke.

"Can I help you?" he asked, counting the boys as if they were dollars.

"We will see," said Mama.

Ike looked around the store from rack to rack to rack. Then, suddenly, he felt his hands get hot and moist. He knew he shouldn't say anything, but he could see a nighttime-blue suit hanging on the third rack. He walked over to it, looked carefully; but none of the suits had price tags. How much? Ike wondered as he touched the sleeve of the blue jacket. Then he touched the jackets next to it. No other suit felt as nice. Ike remembered Mama's instructions. He tried hard to swallow the words "I like it."

But how would Mama know he'd seen a nighttime-blue suit, just like the one he'd dreamed of? Maybe she had heard him say it on the train. But maybe she hadn't! He shifted his weight from one foot to the other. Then before he could stop them, the words sneaked out.

"Mama," he whispered, "I like this blue suit."

Mama raised her eyebrows and pulled the blue suit jacket off the hanger. She rubbed the nighttime-blue material between her thumb and fingers. Ike felt frozen. He couldn't believe what he had done. The boys watched Mama's every move. No one else said a single word.

The shopkeeper, too, waited for Mama to speak. He twisted the hairs on his gray mustache.

Finally, she held the jacket in her fist and her eyes sparkled. Were they sparkling "Mama trouble"? Ike wondered. He had not listened. Not only had he forgotten his bag of garlic on a string, but now he had not done what Mama *said!* He had spoken in the store. He had said "I like it" about a suit. He had even pointed! Ike felt jumpy all over.

At last, Mama spoke to the shopkeeper. "I see only one suit like this," she said. "Must be an odd piece from last year."

"But it is a suit that will wear like iron." The wart on the shopkeeper's nose wiggled more as he spoke louder. "It will last forever, and it costs only seven dollars."

Mama reached into her blouse and took out her purse. She opened it without saying a word. The shopkeeper's eyes bulged at the sight of all those five-dollar bills. Mama closed the purse and pushed the nighttime-blue suit away.

Ike felt a lump growing in his throat. He swallowed. Then, before the shopkeeper could say if, and, or but, Mama handed out suits left and right, saying, "Try on! Try on!" But she gave a boy a suit only after he gave her his string with a bag of garlic attached. "Mustn't smell up the suits," she said.

Ike shivered at the thought of his missing string of garlic while he watched Mama hang each strange necklace on the same hanger.

"A black suit for Ike's friend, Tony," said Mama.

That's just what he wanted, Ike thought.

"A brown suit with stripes for cousin Sol," said Mama, as he handed her his string of garlic.

That's just what he wanted, too, thought Ike. On the train, Ike also had spoken loudly. A blue suit, he'd said. Ike wondered if maybe Mama had heard him. Had he disobeyed without reason, yet? He felt his knees turning to mush. And now, to make matters worse, what would she think when he had no string of garlic to hand her? Ike felt his bare neck as Mama distributed more suits. He leaned on a nearby counter.

"A long blue suit for tall Danny Mantussi. A short black one for cousin Davie. Try on!" Mama said.

The boys scurried to the dressing rooms. Two at a time they stuffed themselves into the two cubicles. They each

hung the hanger with the new suit on a
nail in the wooden wall. Then, as one
boy sat down on the wooden bench to
take off his shoes, another boy closed the
green curtain. The rest of the group

waited near the three-way mirror. The salesman waited there, too, and so did Mama. They all waited as Mama pulled the boy's jacket down or tugged at a sleeve or made the boy bend and stretch. They all waited for the parade and the verdict, a "maybe" or a "put it back," never a "yes."

Oh, how Ike wished someone else would say "I like it." But no one else disobeyed. Soon it would be Ike's turn, and he had no string of garlic to hand Mama. He leaned even harder on the counter. He was feeling weaker every moment.

"How much?" Mama looked at the shopkeeper but pointed to the boys who were carrying suits to try on.

"Seven dollars each," said the gray-haired man.

Mama did not answer. She never did. Moments of silence passed. "We will see," she finally said.

The man looked puzzled. His brow wrinkled and he scratched his head.

At last it was Ike's turn to "try on." Mama reached for the garlic bag. But Ike had no string to hand her. Mama raised her eyebrows, but she slowly took a suit from the rack and held it out for Ike. It was brown.

"Try on," she said.

Ike carried the brown suit as if it were a bag of garbage. But Ike "tried on." Mama *said*. He squeezed into the dressing room with Tony Golida. He hung the suit jacket on the nail and sat down on the wooden bench. Ike squirmed and wriggled as he pulled on the brown pants.

"Oh, no!" he said to Tony. "It's not only brown; it itches and scratches, too. Maybe it won't fit," Ike wished out loud.

～4/Mama's Special Plan

*Ike hated that brown suit even be-*fore he paraded in front of the mirror for Mama. If he had to wear this suit, he would never go outside again. Even if it meant giving up the Sunday-afternoon movie. Ike looked down at his brown suit and squirmed. It itched like a million mosquito bites.

"That fits him like a movie star," the shopkeeper said, with his head studiously tilted to one side.

Yeah, the villain from last week's matinee, thought Ike.

"He looks like a prince," the shopkeeper added, winking at Mama.

But I feel like the itchiest kid on East 136th Street, Ike thought. He wiggled and scratched whenever Mama looked at him.

"All the boys are getting suits?" the shopkeeper asked, and his eyes opened wide with delight.

"We will see," said Mama. "Try on! Try on!" she said to Robert and Patrick in the other dressing room.

Ike was sweating inside this itchy brown suit. It was getting as hot as summer on the roof, he thought.

"Too tight," Mama said. "Put it back."

Ike almost cried when he realized Mama was pointing to Tony's black suit. Mama pulled at two threads on Ike's brown suit jacket. "It wouldn't last," she said. "Put it back." Ike breathed a sigh. He knew he didn't deserve it, but maybe Mama had forgiven him.

She was pointing to two more suits. The shopkeeper took them off the rack and handed them to her. She held the nighttime-blue suit in one hand and a black suit in the other. "Try on!"

Ike reached for the blue suit, feeling worse than ever at having disobeyed such a forgiving Mama. Mama patted Ike's head, but she handed him the black suit.

The blue one she gave to Tony Golida. Tony Golida did not say anything.

Ike tried on the black suit. At least he was out of the itchy brown one, he thought.

"Come on, you guys," Danny Mantussi called. "Let someone else get a turn."

Ike hated the black suit. As he paraded in front of the three-way mirror, he felt as stiff as Joseph Schwartz, the waiter.

"Bend," Mama said. "Stretch," Mama said. Then the verdict.

Ike held his breath, hoping for "put back."

"Maybe," said Mama, pointing to the pile of suits on the counter.

Wouldn't he even get a chance to try on that wonderful nighttime-blue suit? No sooner had he thought it than Mama said, "Just a minute. Let Tony try that black one."

Ike and Tony stepped back into the dressing room. Ike quickly pulled the green curtain shut. Maybe he would get the blue suit, after all, he thought. As he gave Tony the black suit, Tony handed him the blue one. Ike put on the pants. Not even a tickle. He put on the jacket. It felt cool and smooth, like no other suit there, and it even had a silky lining. He walked out to the mirror. In this suit he felt like a prince. He stretched. He bent down. In this handsome holiday suit he paraded with his curly head held high. A once-a-year suit for sure, thought Ike.

"A perfect fit," said the shopkeeper and he poked a sharp finger in Ike's shoulders. "It was made for him."

But Mama was watching Tony, who was strutting as proud as could be in the black suit, but not saying a word. Not saying "I like it."

"A maybe for the black suit," said Mama. Then she looked at Ike. She pulled at the jacket of the nighttime-blue suit. She poked at the collar.

"A beautiful suit," Ike heard the shopkeeper say. "A perfect fit."

"Maybe too perfect," said Mama. "My son will outgrow it before Yom Kippur, could be. Anyway, it's an odd piece. One of a kind must be hard to sell. How much, anyway?"

"Seven dollars, and it comes with

two pairs of pants. A bargain for sure," said the shopkeeper, and he put his arm around Ike's shoulders.

"I wouldn't pay for it, not even a quarter," Mama said.

Ike felt his heart sink into his scuffed-up shoes. He put on his bulky knickers and joined the other boys. He saw the nighttime-blue suit crumpled up under two other suits on the counter.

"So," said Mama, "how much for the other suits?"

"Seven dollars a suit," said the shopkeeper, "but for you, Mrs., I'll not make a penny. For you, I'll say . . . six-fifty."

"Six-fifty a suit?" Mama asked. "For a suit that I can pull hair from the collar? Out of the question. Across the street, even, I could get it for less."

The shopkeeper twisted his mustache. He leaned his elbow on the suits piled up on the counter. "All right, a nice lady like you, so six dollars."

"Six dollars?" said Mama, putting a hand to her heart. "I'm not talking about one suit, you know," and she pointed a pudgy finger at the boys. "Make me a good price like four dollars a suit and I'll buy."

The shopkeeper counted the boys.
"Fourteen suits," he said, "that's another
story. But four dollars, I'd be giving them
away." He scratched his head. "So five-
fifty a suit."

Ike was getting worried. Maybe the
shopkeeper would win and no one would

get a suit. He stood there biting his fingernail. Mama still had not answered.

"Two pairs of pants with each suit, remember," added the shopkeeper.

"Sounds a little better," said Mama, "but I don't mean fourteen suits, five-fifty each. I want thirteen suits, five dollars each." Then she opened her purse and waved the bills. "Talk to the money," she said.

"Five-fifty and not a penny less," said the shopkeeper, waving a finger from side to side.

Mama started walking toward the door. "We go!" she said. One by one the boys started filing out of the shop. Not a word was spoken. Just like Mama had said. When I say we go, we *go.*

Ike felt empty. Even if they came back in, there would only be thirteen suits—for fourteen boys. No suit for me, he thought. No suit for the bigmouth. No suit for the garlic forgetter. He wanted to beg for that blue suit. But this time he made himself listen to Mama. He walked slowly toward the door, listening for more words. Oh, how he wanted that suit.

"Where are you going?" called the shopkeeper, starting to follow Mama and her army. Mama didn't answer right away. Instead she handed each boy his string of garlic—except Ike. Ike felt his face getting red.

The shopkeeper kept calling, "Wait, wait," and he walked after Mama.

Now Mama turned to him. "We are walking with our cash payment to another store," she said.

"You can't do that!" the shopkeeper called, waving his arm frantically. "You're my first customer today. I'll have bad luck all day."

Mama smiled. It was the smile of the winner. She took a few more steps toward the door.

"Please, wait!" the shopkeeper called. "Wait a minute. Let me figure something." He walked back to the counter and took a pencil. Mama stopped walking. The shopkeeper wrote on the back of a brown bag. "Ten suits at cost," he said. "So I'll still make a profit on three and break even on the rest. Or, *oy*, no sale the first sale of the day. Bad luck, yet! Who needs it. So . . . five dollars a suit."

Mama was calm as a just-fed baby. "But remember," Mama said, "if the first sale is a good one, it means good luck all day! So . . . how about four dollars a suit?" She waved the green bills again. Then put them back in her purse.

The shopkeeper started walking away.

"You've got to make a living, too," said Mama. "So thirteen suits five dollars each with an extra pair of pants"—Mama reached into her purse—"and you throw in one suit free."

"One suit free? *Oy.* Let me think," said the shopkeeper, looking at each suit. "So you'll come again next year? You'll bring other customers? . . . All right, thirteen suits, five dollars each, with extra pants and one suit free."

"Good," Mama said. "Now I'll show you the suits we want."

As she pointed a fat finger at the suits, the shopkeeper stuffed them in big bags. It happened so fast, Ike, still peeking from the door and listening, wasn't sure what was going into the bags. But Mama was looking at Ike with a raised eyebrow. He felt angry and worried and sorry, all tied up in a knot.

The other boys were all chattering with excitement as they put their strings of garlic back around their necks.

"A seven-dollar suit for only five dollars. With two pairs of pants, yet! What a clothing maven!" said Joey.

"What an expert!" said Danny Mantussi.

Ike felt his bare neck as he waited for Mama.

5/Mavens

"Ike, hurry," Mama *called from the* doorway. "Help me hand out the bags with each suit in it."

"Coming, Mama." Ike raced through the doorway, into the store.

The shopkeeper scratched his gray head with one hand, and then, after writing the names on the bags, as Mama instructed, he handed bags of suits to Mama and Ike.

"Good day and good luck," Mama said to the shopkeeper.

"With a first sale like this it will be a good day for sure." The shopkeeper beamed. "And maybe next year you will bring *sixteen* boys?"

As Ike and Mama walked out of the

store, the shopkeeper called, "I enjoyed, Mrs! You are one smart buyer!"

Mama smiled.

Then Ike and Mama called the name scribbled on each package. Even the puller-inners watched. Ike handed bags to his first cousins Sammy and Dave. They handed some of the bags to Joey, James Higgins, and Morton Weinstein. Mama handed Tony Golida a bag and he peeked inside it.

"It's the black suit I wanted!" Tony said. "I'll be the handsomest one in church on Easter Sunday."

Mama smiled. "Lucky there was a suit long enough for Danny," Mama said, handing him a bag.

Ike's second cousins Sol and Bernie took their bags and gave their Aunt a kiss on her soft cheek. Herbie and Jack ripped open their bags while Ike still held them.

"It's right!" Jack shouted.

"How did you know which suit I wanted?" called Herbie.

Robert and Patrick came running from down the block when Ike called them. They took their bags breathlessly. "Thanks for taking us, Mrs. Greenberg," said Patrick.

"So," said Mama. "That's thirteen suits, paid for in cash."

Ike's heart pounded. He did not want

to look at Mama's eyes. He knew there was going to be "Mama trouble." He looked at his scuffed-up shoes instead, and shifted his weight from one foot to the other. There would be no nighttime-blue suit to show his friend the fire chief. That much he knew. Then he felt Mama's pudgy finger stroking his chin.

"And here is a bag for my forgetful one." Mama never said anything about the missing string of garlic. Mama didn't have to "say." "You have good taste, Ikey," Mama whispered.

Ike looked up. Mama's eyes were glowing pride, not anger. His hands shook and rattled the brown bag. He opened it as fast as he could.

"Sometimes, Ikey, listening to your heart is more important than listening to Mama. Especially for a first once-a-year suit. Enjoy," said Mama. And she pinched his cheek till it was red.

Ike reached in the bag and pulled out the sleeve . . . of the nighttime-blue suit! All Ike could say was, "Oh, Mama."

"I will soon be listening to *you*," Mama said, and she pushed a lock of hair out of his eye. "You picked out the only mohair suit. And mohair is the best!"

"But Mama, then why did you say the blue suit was odd?" Ike asked.

"That was part of my special plan." Mama smiled. "I had to make the shop-keeper think we'd never want that suit. I had to remind him it was an odd piece. One of a kind. Hard to sell. Then he gave it to us free."

"Would you have known I wanted that suit if I had not said 'I like it'?" Ike asked, trying not to drop the bag. He got nervous just remembering his mistake.

"Of course, Ikey." Mama put her arm around him, but gently, not like a puller-inner. "For once-a-year suits," she added with a grin, "I listen with my eyes. I see the suit you like in your face. But the shopkeeper does not. He is busy see-ing dollars. *That* is my special plan."

Ike smiled at Mama, happy to know Mama's special plan, at last.

"Someday," Mama said, "maybe you will have a clothing store. You are *al-ready* a clothing maven. And everyone listens to a maven, even mamas."

"Now"—Mama got every boy's at-tention with one word—"with one suit free, we have five dollars left over for socks, ties, and even a bellyful of knishes." Then she made her eyes squint seriousness. "Just don't eat so many knishes that you get fat. You must not grow out of your once-a-year suits before you even get home!" Mama laughed. The boys laughed. Ike did, too. He couldn't have been happier as he trailed down Stanton Street after Mama. His first once-a-year suit was the best ever. It was nighttime blue.

And mohair, yet!

About the Author

CAROL SNYDER was born and raised in Brooklyn and attended Brooklyn College. In addition to writing, she teaches children with learning disabilities. Mrs. Snyder lives with her husband, a consulting engineer, and their two children in New Jersey, where the family enjoys community volunteer work, painting, photography, and camping trips.

Ike and Mama and the Once-a-Year Suit is Mrs. Snyder's first book for children.

About the Artist

A native of New Jersey, CHARLES ROBINSON attended Harvard College and the University of Virginia Law School. After practicing law for a number of years, he decided to devote himself full time to his art. He has illustrated over sixty books, including *The Terrible Wave* by Marden Dahlstedt, and he has won the Gold Medal of the Society of Illustrators. Mr. Robinson, his wife, Cynthia, and their three children live in New Vernon, New Jersey.